THE TOPPLING

**A novella by
Cynthia Rumbidzai Marangwanda**

First published in Great Britain in 2025 by:

Carnelian Heart Publishing Ltd
Suite A
82 James Carter Road
Mildenhall
Suffolk
IP28 7DE
UK

www.carnelianheartpublishing.co.uk

Paperback ISBN: 978-1-914287-98-5

E-book ISBN: 978-1-914287-99-2

A CIP catalogue record for this book is available from the British Library.

Editors:
Lazarus Panashe Nyagwambo &
Samantha Rumbidzai Vazhure

Cover design:
Artwork - 'In the embraces of struggle' (2025), by Samantha Rumbidzai Vazhure (Chitende Fine Art)
Layout - Rebeca Covers

Interior:
Typeset by Carnelian Heart Publishing Ltd
Layout and formatting by DanTs Media

To my Creator and Ancestors; for the constant love, guidance,
protection and inspiration. May this be a worthy offering.

"Something fighting floated down from a pale blue sky. As it floated down to my level I saw that it was a black man and a white man locked in the embraces of struggle."

~Dambudzo Marechera, House of Hunger

1

My eyes fly open, and I immediately sense malevolence in the air. I lie motionless on the bed, waiting for my vision to adjust to the dark room. After a short while, I am able to make out a figure standing at the foot of the bed. I reach for the solar lamp on my bedside and switch it on. What faces me is a disconcerting sight. Its form is humanoid, whitish-grey in colour, and it ripples and shimmers like a mirage. It has no discernible features except a pair of glowing orange eyes that seem to brim with venom. I recognise it as the same entity that had been attempting to attack me in the nightmare I just woke from. It has decided to make an appearance in my waking world. The energy emanating from it is nothing good. I let out a heavy sigh – these intrusive visitations are tedious events.

As I am contemplating what to do next, the entity begins to change. I look on, transfixed, as it first takes the shape of a gun which lingers for a short while before transforming into a noose that dangles ominously before me. After a bit of time, it again shifts into the shape of a hammer, before reverting to its humanoid form. I try to make sense of what I am seeing but my mind finds the scene difficult to comprehend.

My daughter, Ruva, is breathing deeply next to me in the bed. She is lost in her own world of dreams, a world which is hopefully more pleasant than the one I just escaped from. Her ten-year-old mind should not be grappling with sinister things in her cocoon of sleep.

As I gingerly move to get out of bed, my uninvited guest makes a sharp hissing sound, stopping me in my tracks. I remain frozen and stare at it for a long, tense moment, unsure what to do. It proceeds to stretch out its hand, as if to grab me, but stops midway. I do not wait to see what it will do next. I stand up, feeling the eyes of my unwanted visitor closely watching every movement I make. I keep expecting it to lunge at me at any moment, but it seems to be exercising restraint, content to merely observe me – at least for now. I move to take the *nhekwe* containing my *bute* from the old chest of drawers next to the bed. The figure promptly advances towards me, and I abort the mission. Having got the hint, I am left with only one other option. With my eyes once more riveted on the intruder, I begin to appeal in a low voice to the benevolent spirits of my lineage for protection and assistance, my voice firm and steady. It is an invocation for them to intervene on my behalf and chase my intruder away. Soon enough, I sense myself slipping into a trance state, entering the liminal space between the land of the living and the realm of those beyond.

***

I have had the ability to see the unseen since I was eleven years old. That was nineteen years ago. The first time it happened, I was seated on a low stool, watching Mother bent over the outside sink as she hand-washed the laundry one ordinary Saturday. She was conversing with our neighbour, Mai Taurai, over the fence. Mai Taurai was sweeping her yard with a straw broom as she talked with

Mother. My job was to help Mother hang the laundry on the clothesline once she was done. Because I was not allowed to participate in the talk between adults, boredom had started creeping up on me. That was when I suddenly noticed an elderly woman standing next to our mango tree. She had milky-white short hair and was dressed in a loose-fitting, dark grey piece of cloth that started just above her bosom and went all the way down to her ankles. Her weathered shoulders were exposed to the elements. I was startled and quickly looked away. I wondered if she was a madwoman who had somehow found her way into our yard. When I nervously looked again, she was still there, gazing at me intently. I gasped, but Mother was too engrossed in her conversation with Mai Taurai to notice. I watched as the woman reached out and beckoned to me. It was too much. I let out a yelp, leapt from the stool and ran to Mother, clinging to her desperately.

"What's wrong MaMoyo? What's got into you?" Mother asked, her voice filled with surprise and confusion.

The name on my birth certificate is not MaMoyo, but my parents had always called me that since I could remember. MaMoyo is the clan name for girls and women of the Moyo or Heart totem in Shona culture. For some peculiar reason, it became my generally accepted name, eventually eclipsing my government name altogether.

"What's going on?" Mai Taurai was curious.

With a trembling finger I pointed to the mango

tree. "Over there."

Mother looked where I was pointing and then back at me. "What's over there?"

"Can't you see the old woman standing there looking at us?"

Mother looked again, longer this time. She shook her head and turned back to me.

"I can't see anyone. You're seeing an old woman? What's she doing?" she asked, concern written all over her face.

"So now these witches are coming for our children in broad daylight? It's hard out here," Mai Taurai chimed in before sighing dramatically.

"She's gesturing for me to come to her," I told Mother, my voice barely above a whisper. I could feel panic making a home in my bones.

"Okay, go in the house and take a nap. Hopefully the old woman will be gone when you wake up." Mother was calm.

"What if she isn't? What if she follows me into the house?"

"Just go and lie down. She's not following you anywhere. I won't allow her to," was Mother's response.

I nodded and did as I was told. I lay buried in my

blankets, trembling furiously, until sleep rescued me. When I woke up nearly two hours later, I scrambled to check if the woman was still there, but she was nowhere in sight. I was beyond relieved. I went back to my room and sat on the bed, feeling confused. Mother walked in and sat next to me.

"Is the old woman still there?" she asked gently. I shook my head.

"Okay. When you saw her, did she feel like a good person or a bad person?"

I thought about it for a moment. "She didn't feel either good or bad. She was just…there."

Mother let out a small sigh, as she put a reassuring arm around my shoulder.

"I sprinkled holy water around the tree as a protective measure. Hopefully it helped," she told me. There was a long pause before she went on. "I hoped I would never have to tell you this, but I also used to see things… inexplicable things when I was about your age. It was really upsetting, and I hated it. As I grew older, the visions only intensified. I would see all sorts of disturbing beings and creatures not of this world, oftentimes dead people. They would try to communicate with me, tell me things and relay messages, but I didn't want to hear any of it; I just wanted to be left in peace. As time passed, it became unbearable. It was not just the visions, people also started to talk, and I began to believe there was something wrong with me. I so desperately wanted to be normal.

"Soon after I gave birth to you, I went to see a famed medicine woman. I feared my unnatural abilities would interfere with my motherhood responsibilities. I was afraid they would get in the way of me being a good mother. I also just wanted to be a regular person. So, I pleaded with the medicine woman to rid me of my affliction. She was very reluctant to help me at first; she insisted I was gifted rather than cursed, but I didn't want to hear it. I kept pleading with her until she finally caved in. She gave me a concoction that would permanently suppress the visions I saw, but it came at a price. I wouldn't be able to have any more children. It was an excruciating dilemma because I absolutely revelled in being a parent, but I was so tired of being abnormal. I spent days swinging back and forth between wanting to ingest it and wanting to throw it away. Eventually my desire to lead a normal life won and I took it.

"The concoction worked; I never saw those terrible things again. I was so relieved because I thought it was behind me for good, but it seems you have inherited my curse. The thought of it is absolutely devastating to me. I hate to think of you going through what I went through, of you seeing and experiencing similar things to what I did. There isn't much I can do to help you at this time, because you're still so young. You have to endure it until you're old enough to find a solution, like I did. For now, I advise you to turn to Jesus Christ and prayer. The Lord will shield and protect you until you can free yourself from this bondage. I will pray for you and ask fellow prayer warriors from church to do the same. I'm so very sorry my dear."

I sat there for a long while without saying anything, trying to process what Mother had just told me. It was overwhelming for my young brain to absorb. I felt numb and shell-shocked.

"How do you feel about this?" Mother's voice was gentle.

I tried to answer but no words came out. I could only shake my head. Mother sighed deeply, stood up and left the room. I could see the heaviness on her shoulders as she walked away.

A few days later, I was seated in my classroom at school. It was lunchtime and I had just finished consuming the contents of my lunchbox. The boy who sat next to me was animatedly telling me about his mischievous antics at home the day before, but I was paying him scant attention. I glanced out the window and froze. Peering through the window were a lion and lioness. They seemed to be searching for something in our classroom. When the male lion's eyes landed on me, it proceeded to unleash an astonishing roar, and I in turn let out a hysterical scream, startling and panicking my classmates. Within moments, a teacher had bounded into the class to ascertain what was happening, but all I could do was shake uncontrollably and point at the window.

I was eventually escorted to the Headteacher's office, where I calmed down enough to explain what I had seen. After listening to my account, I could see she was quite taken aback and not sure what to make of it. She wasted no time calling Mother and explaining what had happened. After the phone call she told me to go home and rest and gave me a few days off from school. I was driven home in the school truck.

From then on, seeing strange visions became the norm for me. Sometimes what I saw was benign, other times it took on more sinister forms. I also started having vivid dreams drenched in heavy symbols and imagery that I struggled to wrap my head around. At home I was embraced as I was and never made to feel like I was flawed in any way, but the outside world was more complex. Some were fascinated by me, while others fell anywhere between being uncomfortable and believing I was deranged, even going as far as swearing I was demon-possessed. I learned to question my own sanity from then on. I went from being a carefree child to being withdrawn, gloomy, and solitary in a very brief space of time. I felt bizarre and defective, so I retreated into myself. I did not wait for society to make me a pariah, I did it on my own.

A few months after the incident at school, I was walking home with my parents after visiting a relative who lived in the same high-density suburb of Dzivarasekwa, on the western side of Harare. As we were about to turn the corner onto our street, a man approached us. He was bald and dressed in a loose white garment and sandals. From his dressing, it was clear he was a member of the Vapositori, the umbrella term for the numerous African indigenous churches whose adherents worship out in the open and practice mystical faith healing, often combining elements of African spirituality and Christian beliefs. I noticed a dazzling orb of light that seemed to be following him.

"Excuse me. Apologies for approaching you in the street like this," the man addressed my parents. "My angel instructed me to pass on a message to you, if you will allow me." He gestured to the orb of light as he said this, and I deduced that it was the angel being referred to.

"You may go ahead," said Father, one eyebrow raised.

"Thank you. I will get straight to the point. Your daughter here has a great and rare gift. She is not like most people; she is set apart and has a special anointing on her. This child of yours has the sacred eye and sacred heart. She possesses high intelligence and is blessed with deep knowledge, the kind of knowledge that is natural, innate, and effortless. She is meant to tear down strongholds of false supremacy. But as much as her gift is a blessing, it also has its shadow side. The purity of her powers makes her an attractive target for the princes of this world and their forces. A gift like hers makes her vulnerable. Protect and guard her. Cherish her. She is liberation personified," he intoned.

The three of us were lost for words. Eventually, Father cleared his throat and said, "Thank you for the message. We appreciate it and it has been received."

Father raised his hands and pressed both palms

together in a gesture of gratitude to the man. The messenger nodded in acknowledgement and walked away without another word, his bright orb in tow.

"Do you think what he said is true?" I asked, as we watched him leave.

"Time will tell my dear," was Mother's answer.

I desperately wanted to believe the message I had just heard, but I was filled with doubt. I did not feel gifted or anointed. I felt gravely unlucky and haunted. As the days and weeks passed, I gradually convinced myself that the encounter with the man and his angelic shadow was no more than a random occurrence that held no real merit, and thus was not to be taken seriously.

In an effort to cope with the relentless visions that pursued me, I eventually took Mother's advice and threw myself into the Christian faith when I was thirteen. As I daily imbibed biblical scripture, my belief in the gospel became a refuge in a confounding world. I told myself the blood of Christ was my protective armour and source of strength. My zeal for the Holy Ghost helped me deal with the myriad other ghosts that populated my world. Although it did not chase them away, it made their presence bearable. My faith was a solace and soothing sanctuary that I gratefully escaped to, until one hot October day two years later.

I was looking for something to eat after school in the kitchen at home when my sight suddenly went dark. I felt myself sinking into an irresistible river of nothingness. Mother was taking a break from her seamstress duties and walked into the kitchen at that very moment. She later told me she watched in horror as I experienced severe seizures before losing consciousness and collapsing. Mother rushed to the telephone in our living room and called the workshop where Father worked as a carpenter. Father rushed home in a work vehicle, and they ferried me to the nearest public hospital. I regained consciousness on my way there, but I was unable to talk and could not move the lower half of my body.

On arrival at the hospital, I was sent to the casualty ward. When the doctor showed up, he examined me before instructing me to get a CT scan so a clearer picture of the problem could be ascertained. I lay there, mute and helpless, having to rely on hand gestures and writing to communicate. When the scan results came back, the doctor told us he could not find anything wrong or pinpoint a cause for my mysterious ailment. I listened to him suggest that I be taken to a neurologist who might be of more assistance in my case. My parents looked small and lost as they sombrely took in the doctor's words. I could see the anxiety visibly etched on their faces, and I felt sorry for them. I was their only child; I was all they had. All three of us were stranded in a wilderness of uncertainty. I felt a vivid despair lodge in my throat and refuse to vacate the premises.

I was discharged from the hospital the next day, still unable to speak, still crippled. I was going back home a voiceless invalid who had to be pushed around in a second-hand wheelchair. I had no idea if I would ever regain my ability to walk and talk again. I once more tried to find hope and strength in my Lord and Saviour, but the personal purgatory I found myself in was too burdensome. My faith was overwhelmed by my sorrow.

A few days after I was back home, my parents took me to see the neurologist. After running some tests and examining me thoroughly, she also concluded she could not ascertain what was wrong with me. This left us at a loss and clueless as to how to proceed. The fragile hope I had been clinging to all but died. Outside the neurologist's office tears began to stream from my eyes.

"Don't worry MaMoyo. We will find a way to get you healed. Everything will be fine in the end," Mother said tenderly, wiping the wetness from my cheeks. I nodded and tried to smile but failed.

Three weeks later, I was lying in bed just after midday, my mind blank. I was beyond the point of despondency, utterly numb. I suddenly felt a cool breeze waft through my room followed by a powerful gust of wind. I stirred uncomfortably, not sure what was happening. In no time, the room was covered in thick mist. I was about to reach for the hand bell on my bedside to ring for Mother when two forms began to materialise in the mist. I watched, mesmerised, as the forms became clearer.

The first form crystallised into a man dressed in a black and white cowhide loincloth reaching his knees and a *ngundu* of black feathers crowning his head. I could tell by his facial features that he was of advanced age, but he appeared strong and fit. The second was someone I immediately recognised; it was the elderly woman I had seen standing next to the mango tree when I was eleven, my very first vision. She looked exactly the same as she had that day, except this time, she was smiling at me. The man stepped forward and addressed me.

"I am Tateguru, the original founder of your father's lineage. I am your progenitor. With me is Muchembere, my principal wife and your foremother," he said, gesturing to the elderly woman.

"We have come to set you free from what oppresses you," Tateguru continued. "But before we can do that, there is something you must take heed of. You are not meant to embrace the coloniser's religion or beliefs. You are called to follow and practice the ancient way. Yours is the path of tradition, to walk in the footsteps of those that have gone before you. You are meant to reclaim your origins as a child of this soil, to mine the past in order to create a golden future. Your salvation cannot be found in alien beliefs, because it already courses through your blood and resides in your bones. It lives within you; it cannot be given to you by an outsider. You contain generations upon generations of power. All the guidance and assistance you need can be accessed through us, your departed elders. You never journey alone. The coloniser's faith is not for you. This is why you are suffering in this way, because you have gone against your nature. Before we can free you, you must agree to renounce the invader's religion and never claim it again. Will you do this?" His voice was firm but kind.

I knew I had no option, so I nodded my head with vigour.

Muchembere stepped forward. She exuded a warm, maternal energy that instantly made me feel safe. I realised I should never have been afraid of her that first time she appeared to me.

"You have done well my beloved seed. You are healed now. Your speech is restored, and your legs are functional once more." In that moment a sensation akin to an electric surge ripped through my body, and I let out a sharp cry. The mist instantly evaporated along with Muchembere and Tateguru. My room was back to its dull self.

I attempted to lift my left leg and was shocked when it actually complied. I sat up stiffly and swung both legs from the bed to the floor. It felt unnatural. I got to my feet, unsteady, and walked out to find Mother. She was sitting on a sofa in the living room, darning some clothes.

"Mhamha, look!" She nearly fainted.

***

A deep shudder ripples through my body, and I feel myself coming out of the trance state. I am in the process of thanking my ancestors and spirit guardians when a small voice says, "Mhamha, the scary ghost is gone."

I look over at the bed in surprise. Ruva is sitting up, looking at me wide-eyed.

"Ruva? I thought you were asleep!" I exclaim sharply. "You saw that thing standing there?"

"Yes, I did. I think it wanted to eat me. But when you were praying, you took your special stick and pointed it at the creepy ghost, and it disappeared. You saved me Mhamha."

I am briefly confused before it dawns on me that Ruva has just narrated what happened while I was in the trance. The 'special stick' is my *tsvimbo*, my wooden ritual staff. I had it made a few years ago, after being told by Tateguru in a dream that I needed my own staff. Tateguru directed me to the old man who carved it for me and gave me instructions on its design and which symbols to put on it, particularly the bull's head on the top, which represents my clan's totem animal.

"It wasn't after you Ruva, I was the one it wanted. But it's gone now, no need to worry about it anymore," I try to reassure her but she does not seem convinced.

I get back in the blankets with her.

"You can sleep now, everything is okay," I tell her, turning off the lamp. There is wetness in my eyes as I lie next to her. Her name Ruva means 'flower'. I have burdened my beautiful flower with an eye that perceives disturbing things, things that can potentially wilt her petals. My guilt is immense.

I met Ruva's father when I was eighteen. My own father died a few days shy of my seventeenth birthday from undiagnosed diabetes. One day, he was alert and going about his normal business, the next day he was in a diabetic coma that he never woke from. The night before Father died, I had a dream of him waving at me as he got onto an unmarked bus before it drove off. The grief I experienced after his passing was unbearable. I spent days stumbling around in a state of shock, my eyes blurry with tears. Neither I nor Mother could comfort each other; we were both reeling from the weight of our loss and bereavement. Our pillar had crumbled, and the space Father had occupied was now a gaping void.

As a way of lightening the financial load on Mother, I decided to start working so I could take care of my own upkeep. Mother tried vigorously to dissuade me, urging me instead to continue with school and assuring me she could manage, but I was resolute. I already had no desire to remain in school because I was an outcast among my peers. I struggled to relate to them because I was always too engrossed with the visions and unworldly insights that stalked me day and night. My schoolmates found me strange and impossible to comprehend, and I was regularly taunted and ridiculed. I became accustomed to snide remarks and insults directed at my person. I had no friends. Ostracism was my norm. The teachers were hardly any kinder. For this reason, even though I was an exceptional student, I found school a generally hostile environment. I left it behind with no remorse after completing my Ordinary Level studies.

At the ripe age of seventeen, I entered the Zimbabwean workforce and became one of the precariously employed masses of the land. I found work waitressing in restaurants and hotels, or stocking shelves and serving customers in supermarkets and shops in and around Harare. Even though the money was not much, I enjoyed being able to cover my own expenses and helping out Mother when needed.

It was while working at an upmarket dining establishment in the affluent northern suburbs one evening, that I first encountered Ruva's father. He was dining with friends, and I was assigned to serve their table.

"What's your name, gorgeous girl? I love your complexion. You're a real black beauty, aren't you? Very enticing," he flirted as I took his order.

"Thank you sir. I go by MaMoyo," I replied flatly.

Men hitting on me while waitressing was something I was used to. It was a hazard of the job which I never took seriously.

"Ah, today is my lucky day. Moyo women are the sweetest. A fine girl like you shouldn't be doing such work. Let me pay bride-price for you and change your life," his offer was playful.

"I'm flattered but I'm quite capable of changing my own life, thank you," I told him before walking off.

By the time my shift ended at midnight I had forgotten this small exchange. As I headed out to the car park to get onto the staff van that would take us home, I heard someone call my name. I stopped and looked around to find someone running up behind me. It was the man who had tried to flirt with me earlier. I let out a sigh.

"How can I help you sir?" I asked glibly.

"No need to be so formal, babe. I want to be your friend. We can be best friends, you and I. Just give me a chance beautiful girl," he eyed me lasciviously.

I rolled my eyes. "A chance to do what exactly? Sleep with me and discard me after you're done?"

He shook his head vehemently. "A chance to get to know you. You can start by letting me drive you home."

"No thank you sir. Now allow me to be on my way."

"No, I won't allow you. I never take no for an answer, especially from a beauty like you. If you won't let me drive you home, then I'll just follow you all the way to your house," the man said with a determined tone.

This both surprised and irritated me. "Are you serious? Doesn't that strike you as stalker behaviour? I'm not interested, full stop," I was firm with him.

"Are you really not interested, or are you just playing hard to get? Either way, I'll do what's necessary to get you interested. I'm not letting a gem like you slip through my fingers."

I was exasperated, but I could tell he meant what he was saying. He was not going to let me go. I decided to take the risk and capitulated.

"Alright. But you better not try anything funny."

"You're a feisty little thing, aren't you? I like that," he said with a grin as he led me to his expensive European car. Reluctantly, I followed him

On our way, he asked me the usual questions about myself, but I answered with scant detail. He then proceeded to tell me about himself, even though I was not keen to know. He told me he went by the name Boss Pfuti, which was shortened to Boss P. The fact that he was nicknamed after a firearm made me frown. He had apparently started out working for the dreaded state intelligence organisation as an intelligence officer, but he was now a gold dealer, and he had a number of other business ventures. He refused to divulge his age, but it was clear he was no longer in his twenties. He proudly informed me he was very well-connected in the corridors of power and was therefore untouchable.

"Good for you," I said sarcastically. "Now, about

you working for the state intelligence organisation. Did you know it was born out of the Special Branch of the British South Africa Police? It only became the state intelligence organisation that we know now after independence, but its roots are in Rhodesia."

He glanced at me with an amused expression. "You're clever too? The whole package I see."

"Not so much clever, but rather a lover of history," I explained matter-of-factly.

When we arrived at my home, Boss P parked by the gate and turned to me.

"Since I already know where you live, you might as well give me your phone number, so I can keep in touch with you easily."

"You're relentless," I said.

"When I want something, I don't give up until I get it. It's one of my biggest strengths."

"It could be a strength, or it could be a toxic trait, depending on how you look at it. Anyway, I'll give you my number because I clearly don't have a choice," I felt weary. After getting my phone number, he drove off a happy man, and I was left perturbed.

That night, Muchembere appeared in my dream looking uncharacteristically worried, but I did not think much of it. Boss P immediately began bombarding me with phone calls, surprise visits both at home and at work, and lavish gifts. To say I was overwhelmed is an understatement. It was a lot to handle for my teenage self, especially since I found him largely unimpressive and unstimulating. His persistence paid off, however, as I felt my heart beginning to thaw and my will softening towards him as the days progressed. Despite myself, I began to develop feelings for this man who had inserted himself into my world without being invited in. This both confused and troubled me for a while, but I eventually succumbed to what I was feeling for him. When I told Mother about the strong emotions brewing within me for Boss P, she was not thrilled.

"Be careful of these men about town and their fast lives. It rarely ends well with such types," she cautioned, but I was already in the process of falling headlong for Boss P, so I brushed aside her advice.

A couple of months into our relationship, Boss P suggested that I move out of Mother's house and have my own place where we could meet and relax freely. He proceeded to rent me a garden flat in The Avenues, which I promptly moved into. He also told me to quit working because he would take care of all my needs, which I did without hesitation. At this point I was completely besotted with him and believed I had found the love of my life. My days became a heady whirlwind that revolved around my relationship with Boss P. Life was glittering and exciting.

It only lasted eight months.

One day, I received a phone call from a woman who informed me that she was Boss P's wife of twelve years. She told me they had three children together and had no plans to separate or divorce. She also told me that I should not think I was special to Boss P.

"There have been girls before you, and there will be others after. He uses girls like you for fun. It's his pattern. You are nothing more than a pawn to him. Enjoy it while it lasts," she said before hanging up.

In that moment it felt like I could not breathe. I sank to the floor, suddenly devoid of energy. It confirmed my initial negative feelings about Boss P when we first met, and my disinterest in being involved with him in the beginning. The realisation that I was nothing more than a 'small house', a mistress, was humiliating. To think I had been envisioning myself getting married and starting a family with a philanderer, and now those dreams lay in shambles around me. It was hardly surprising that a man of his age and means had a wife and children. I had been naïve to think otherwise. I recalled Mother's warning about him and broke down in wracking sobs. I was gutted. I felt adrift and betrayed.

When Boss P came to see me that night, he found my bags packed. I told him about the call I had received from his wife. I then informed him that I wanted nothing more to do with him, and our relationship was done.

He sneered on hearing this. His face changed and

took on what can only be described as a demonic countenance. He no longer resembled himself; he looked infernal. I felt waves of fear crashing through me. My body began to tremble.

"You think you can leave me just like that you little whore! After everything I have done for you? Do I look like the type you can just walk away from? You must be out of your immature mind. You're not going anywhere. You're staying right here for as long as I want you to!" he barked at me.

I was stunned. Was this the same man who had been treating me like I was his entire world just yesterday? Who was this person saying these horrible things to me? Was this a clone? I watched in horror as he pulled out a pistol from under his jacket and pointed it at me.

"If you insist on doing anything stupid, I won't hesitate to use this. And I won't get in trouble for it either. There haven't been any consequences before, and there won't be any now. I told you I was untouchable. And if you try to run away, I will easily find you, I have eyes everywhere. Now take off your clothes," his command was cold as ice.

I did as I was told with tears flowing. He raped me that night, and many nights after that. I was nothing more than a sex slave to him from that moment on. Life went from delightful to deeply hellish, literally overnight. It felt like a soulless monster had imprisoned me in a dungeon and thrown away the key. I desperately told Mother what was happening over the phone, but she was powerless to help. She told me Boss P had paid her a visit and threatened her as well. She could only pray for a miracle on my behalf. So I sat in that garden flat day after day, at the mercy of my lover-turned-captor.

After some weeks, I noticed my period had not appeared when it normally should. Alarm bells went off in my mind. I did not want to believe the unthinkable had happened, that I was possibly pregnant by this man I had come to loathe and fear. I decided it was best not to tell him about my suspicions because I was not sure what his reaction would be. His behaviour had grown increasingly erratic, and he regularly flew into violent fits of rage over the slightest things. News of a potential pregnancy might trigger the worst in him, and I was not ready to deal with that. By that point I was not allowed to venture out by myself or meet with other people, so there was no way of accessing a pregnancy test. He kept me under constant surveillance and tracked my movements. I could only wait.

A few days later, I was lying listlessly on the leather sofa, trying and failing to watch television. The images and sounds were not registering in my mind, and I was dissociated from my surroundings. A strong earthy scent suddenly wafted into my nostrils. It was so strong I sat up, trying to figure out where it was coming from. Then I watched in surprise as Muchembere materialised in front of me. I was so happy to see her, I promptly burst into tears. I scrambled up and rushed to kneel before her oasis-like presence.

She looked down at me with a pained expression.

"I am hurting for you little one. Fate took you down a dangerous road. You are still so young and inexperienced. That wicked man took advantage of your vulnerability and lured you into his crocodile's lair, and now you are trapped. It is his habit unfortunately. He sold his soul a long time ago; he is into sorcery and evil magic. He preys on spiritually gifted young women. He detects them by their aura, pursues them, and draws them into his depraved world using manipulation and coercion to get his way. He then feeds off their energy to gain luck, wealth, and power. After getting what he wants, he kills them and finds the next victim.

"He usually targets young women with *njuzu* mermaid spirits and underwater gifts that are not fully developed and harnessed yet, but in your case, he could not resist the brightness of your aura, even though your type of spiritual essence of an ethereal nature, is not what he is usually drawn to. And that was his mistake because he will soon experience our wrath. He will pay for what he has done to you. Worry not child, all will be taken care of." She paused and when I looked up, I saw her smiling at me. "I can see you have a seed germinating within you. A most beautiful flower. Keep in mind that although the father is monstrous, the flower itself is innocent. Do not conflate the two. I must go now." Without giving me a chance to say anything, she evaporated as suddenly as she had appeared.

I was left to digest what Muchembere had said. Instead of feeling dismayed about the pregnancy that she had all but confirmed, I unexpectedly felt intense maternal feelings rising within me. This made me feel confused and conflicted. I truly despised Boss P, but I somehow felt protective of the child he had fathered that was now growing in my womb. Even though I still felt uncertain about what lay ahead, I found I was no longer consumed with dread and anxiety. I trusted that it was all in my ancestors' hands and they would deal with it.

The next day, Boss P passed by to see me in the morning. He was in a particularly bad mood, so I tried my best not to upset him further, but it was futile. At a certain point he just snapped and started slapping me repeatedly. When the slaps turned into punches, I ran into the bathroom and locked the door. I listened in sheer terror as he bellowed and cursed and threw things for what seemed an eternity before he finally left. When I eventually unlocked the door and stepped out of the bathroom, it felt like I had just been through a near-death experience.

Sleep evaded me that night, so I took my cell phone and started scrolling through social media to distract myself. I had been scrolling for what seemed like ages, when I came across a headline on one of the major tabloid pages that made me freeze. It read: BREAKING NEWS! WEALTHY GOLD DEALER & BUSINESSMAN BOSS PFUTI INVOLVED IN FATAL ACCIDENT! Underneath the headline was a file photo of Boss P grinning and holding a bottle of champagne, in what looked like a nightclub. With trembling fingers, I clicked the attached link to read the full story.

He had apparently been in a head-on collision with another vehicle. According to the article, the impact of the crash was so severe that it instantly decapitated him. I gasped. With him in the car was a young model who had also died, though not as gruesomely as he did. I was stunned. I felt chills all over my body. I was so shocked that I found myself doubting whether what I had just read was true. Was my jailer and abuser really gone for good? It slowly dawned on me that this was actually real, and not a creation of my embattled mind. My ancestors had intervened on my behalf and eliminated him. He had paid the ultimate price for his mistreatment of me.

There was not a single shred of grief or sadness anywhere in my being. There was shock, and there was overwhelming relief. My ordeal was finally over. I was free. I felt like ululating with joy. I knelt on the floor and offered my ancestors an impassioned prayer of thanksgiving. Afterwards, I called Mother and told her the news. She was so relieved she wept.

"I thought the next time I would see you, you would be in a coffin," she told me, sobbing.

"Well, you're going to see me very soon. I'm coming home," I said.

I packed my belongings, took one last look at that godforsaken flat, and walked out to reacquaint myself with freedom. It was not a pleasant journey home because I was wracked with anxiety the whole way. I kept expecting one of Boss P's minions to suddenly appear and take me back into captivity. But nothing of the sort happened, and I made it home safely. Mother welcomed me back with open arms. When I told her about my pregnancy and my decision to keep the baby, she was taken aback but ultimately understanding. Seven-and-a-half months later, Ruva arrived in the world.

2

I wake up at daybreak and take a quick bath. When I am done, I take out Ruva's school uniform before going to check on Mother in her room. She is still sleeping. She is no longer the strong, energetic woman of my younger years. She was infected with coronavirus during the COVID-19 pandemic three years ago and nearly lost her life. She spent two weeks in the intensive care unit before miraculously rallying and recovering. Although Mother eventually overcame the worst parts of the disease, she was left with lingering after-effects that refuse to resolve, ailments like intense fatigue, headaches, shortness of breath and bodily aches. In addition, she also suffers from hypertension. When I am at work, I have asked the neighbours to check on her. On the days she feels better, she sits at her sewing machine and makes clothes and outfits for clients, but this happens intermittently.

I wake Ruva up to go bath, and while she shuffles to the bathroom I get dressed. I wear my regular clothes; I will change into my waitress uniform at work. I tie my forest of natural hair into a tight ponytail, reminding myself I should get it plaited soon. When Ruva is done bathing, she puts on her school uniform and goes to eat her cereal. I go and check on Mother again and find her now awake, sitting up in bed.

"*Mangwanani*. How did you sleep?" I greet her.

"Morning my daughter. I slept okay except for

some pain in my joints. And you, how did you sleep?"

"I slept well. About to head to work now," my response is breezy. No mention of my previous night's intrusive visitor.

Ruva walks in and greets her grandmother with a hug. Mother dotes on Ruva, and she in turn adores Mother. Their bond is heart-warming to behold. The two of us say goodbye to Mother and head out, first to Ruva's school which is a short distance from our house. My life essentially revolves around my little family at home and my job. I have no social life to speak of. I leave Ruva at the gate and head for the nearby bus stop to wait for a *kombi*. In no time, a brightly painted one arrives, and I get in. I sit at the very back and take note of the other passengers. Everyone is absorbed in their own galaxy, a dozen Milky Ways in one vehicle. The driver is playing popular Zim dancehall songs at high volume, and I nod along to the music.

Thirty minutes later, the kombi stops at a bus rank in the busy central business district, and we all disembark. It is a balmy day. We are in late September, the season of *pfumvudza* – springtime, when nature is reborn in all its colour and liveliness after the slumber and torpor of winter. This is the time of year when the striking purple flowers of Harare's famous jacaranda trees bloom. It is a mesmerising sight to behold. Each year I find myself awed by the purple beauty of the jacarandas, but I am also conflicted. I am aware that jacaranda trees are an invasive species introduced by colonial settlers, and they stifle the growth of indigenous tree species. Jacaranda trees are beguiling colonial relics; highly aesthetically appealing yet insidious. My enjoyment of them is laced with guilt.

After a short walk from the bus rank, I arrive at my workplace – the five-star M Hotel situated in the heart of Harare's city centre. The hotel has been a landmark of the city since it was founded in the early 1900s by a Scottish settler who apparently built his wealth from looting massive amounts of cattle from the local African population. I have been working as a waitress here for four years now. Today, the hotel is hosting a luncheon for a visiting Commonwealth delegation that is here as part of Zimbabwe's ongoing efforts to rejoin the association after the former president withdrew the country in 2003 due to disagreements. I will be one of the waiters serving the delegates and local government officials. On arrival, I politely greet my workmates and ready myself for the busy day ahead.

Soon after one p.m., the luncheon begins, and I find myself immersed in the business of serving and catering to the domestic and international powers-that-be. Halfway through the luncheon, I notice a European man standing by himself at the back of the room. He looks vaguely familiar, although I have no clue where I might know him from. I conclude that he is most likely one of the Commonwealth delegates, but I wonder why he has removed himself from the rest of the group. I stop to study him. He appears and feels anachronistic. His clothes look dated, almost as if he stepped right out of Victorian

England, and I find myself wondering why he is dressed in that manner. Despite his attire, he has a very proud bearing, almost haughty. As I am assessing him, I realise that his eyes are trained on me. I quickly look away and carry on with my duties.

For the rest of the luncheon, I keep stealing glances at the strange man. He does not move from his position or attempt to join the rest of the dignitaries. I find my focus wandering to him so much he becomes almost a distraction.

I end up asking a fellow waiter what he thinks of the odd man standing on his own at the back of the room.

"What man are you talking about? I don't see anyone there," is my colleague's response as he looks around in confusion.

A shiver runs down my spine. If the strange man at the back is not visible to my workmate, then it can only mean one thing; he is an apparition that only I can see. When I glance again at the back of the room to study him more closely, I find no one there. I let out a heavy sigh and continue with the business at hand.

As I go to sleep that night, thoughts of the ghostly man at the luncheon haunt me. I am now accustomed to seeing spirits, but something about this one feels significant. When I do eventually go to sleep, Tateguru appears in my dream. He hands me a *gano*.

"You are meant to right the wrongs of history.

Always keep in mind that your spirit is the most potent weapon. With it, you can slay any enemy or oppressor," he tells me as I accept the proffered ritual battle axe.

The following morning, I wake up and go about my usual routine. Even though it is a weekend, Ruva wakes up with me, and proceeds to go play outside with her dolls and toys in our small yard. Mother is also up early, and she is sitting outside, soaking up the morning sun. As I am getting ready, Ruva suddenly comes bounding into the house, looking agitated.

"Mhamha, there is a white man standing at our gate," she says breathlessly.

I feel a rush of blood to my head, and my heart begins to pound. Even before going outside, I know who she is referring to.

"Okay, let's go and see," I say nervously, taking her hand in mine.

We meet Mother at the door, coming in. She looks worried.

"Ruva said she saw someone or something at the gate. What's going on?"

"That's what we're going to check now."

When we step outside, my suspicions are confirmed. Through the grille gate, one can easily see someone standing on the other side, and it is indeed the unusual man from the luncheon. He looks exactly the way he did yesterday when I saw him. The day is warm, but an icy draft seems to be radiating from his general direction. Ruva and I stand there staring at him, unsure what to do.

I am startled when he unexpectedly raises his hand and says, "Greetings!"

Neither of us respond. I turn to Ruva and tell her to get her stuff and go into the house; I want to talk to the man alone. When I turn back towards the gate, there is no one there. I feel an odd mixture of relief and disappointment. I go back in the house and inform Mother about what Ruva and I had seen. I also tell her that I saw the same person at the hotel luncheon yesterday.

She looks perturbed. "I'm tired of these phantoms and goblins always following you. Now they are following Ruva too. I don't like it at all. Why won't these things just leave us alone so we can lead normal lives?" Mother asks no one in particular and sounds upset.

"I've made peace with the fact that a so-called normal life is not for me. I just hate that Ruva is also burdened. Anyway, let me go to work or I'll be late," I say to her.

After saying goodbye to Ruva and telling her not to worry about the white man she saw at the gate, I head to work. I try not to think about the incident that just occurred at home. When I reach the hotel, I blink furiously in disbelief. Standing right in front of the entrance is the same man who was at our gate earlier. It is starting to feel like everywhere I turn he is there. I toy with the idea of ignoring him and simply walking past, but something tells me to engage him instead.

I stop in front of him and say, "Hello. Can I help you?" in a clipped voice.

His grey eyes meet mine, and I once again get the overwhelming feeling that I know him from somewhere.

"We meet again. How are you faring this fine day in Salisbury?" he asks pleasantly.

"Salisbury?" I ask with raised eyebrows. "That name hasn't been in use since 1982. It's called Harare now."

"How ridiculous. Why would anyone call it such a ghastly name? Salisbury it is and Salisbury it shall remain," he states.

I look at him in amusement before saying, "So I guess you won't be pleased to know that this land is no longer Rhodesia either. It's now Zimbabwe, the great house of stone! In fact, Rhodesia is dead and buried."

His face pales a shade more than it already was.

"Dead? What an erroneous assumption. Rhodesia will never die. Rhodesia is very much alive now, as it was before," he declares.

"Is that so? Who are you anyway?" I ask.

"My name is Cecil."

I am about to ask him to further elucidate when realisation strikes me like a thunderbolt. I inhale sharply.

"No way," I say, with a slightly shaky voice. "Cecil as in Cecil John Rhodes, the notorious British arch-imperialist?"

He nods proudly. "Indeed, it is I."

I stand there with my mouth open, staring at him. I have interacted with plenty of dead people in my life, but conversing with the architect of my country's colonisation is another level of encounter.

"Okay. So, what are you doing here, and what do you want with me?" I finally manage to ask.

"Take a stroll with me," Cecil says and begins walking.

I am debating whether to follow him or go to work when a disembodied voice says, "Walk with him". I know better than to disobey, so I scurry after Cecil. We cross the street, headed towards the open square overlooked by M Hotel. We pass the flower-sellers at its margins and enter its grounds.

"Ah, the lovely Cecil Square, named after yours truly!" He sounds delighted.

I make a face. "It was called Cecil Square back then.

It's known as Africa Unity Square now.".

It is now his turn to make a face. "Who keeps giving these places such hideous names? But then again, judging by the square's current state, the new name is more apt. Its decrepitude aside, this space holds great significance in Rhodesian history. Cecil Square is one of the very first places where my Pioneer Column raised the mighty British flag as they annexed Mashonaland for the British Empire. I am sure you are aware that the square was designed to resemble the Union Jack. Such ingenuity and patriotism are extremely admirable. I am glad to see the original design has stood the test of time," he says.

"It's rather odd calling them the Pioneer Column, isn't it? 'Pioneer' means 'first' and how could they be the first in a land that was already long inhabited? Should have called it the Invader Column or Occupier Column or something along those lines," I muse.

"What you're saying is irrelevant. These were great men and founders who brought civilisation and progress to these backward lands," Cecil says.

"How do you define backward? Before your motley band of settler mercenaries arrived, this land had a functional, thriving society and economy, and it was developing as it should. Then you people came, and look at it now. Unstable, confused, bedevilled by problems. What you brought was certainly nothing civilised or progressive. And if there's anything irrelevant around here, that would be you Cecil!" I retort.

He stops and says indignantly, "My dear native girl, I am as relevant now as I ever was. Maybe even more so. Your so-called Zimbabwe is the offspring of Rhodesia. I birthed your country, and this is a fact."

"My dear unrepentant arch-colonialist, I am not your native girl. I don't appreciate being referred to in that manner. I am MaMoyo, and you may refer to me as such. In fact, I insist you do," I say firmly.

He merely purses his lips and continues walking. I notice that the people around us do not seem to be aware of both Cecil's and my presence. Cecil being invisible to the average person is not surprising but what of me? A woman seemingly talking to herself animatedly in public would surely be noticeable. But it appears I have also ceased to be visible to those in the physical world. It is as if Cecil and I are in our own parallel world that everyone else cannot access, a world somehow within the ordinary world, but energetically separate from it. I find this quite bizarre.

"Where is the proof of your continued relevance Cecil? Or Rhodesia's? Show me unequivocally how the empire still lives and reigns in post-colonial Zimbabwe," I challenge him.

"That prefix is very misplaced. There is nothing 'post-colonial' about this land we walk on. I am very happy to show you proof because it is abundant," he says with confidence.

Cecil stamps his foot, and we instantaneously find ourselves in front of one of the main cathedrals in the city centre. To say I am surprised is an understatement. I look around in wild confusion.

"What just happened? How did we get here?"

"Being dead comes with its own set of perks and benefits. Count yourself lucky to experience some of them before your time."

He turns his attention to the cathedral. It is large and authoritative, even a bit intimidating.

"Glorious, isn't it?" he says, admiration written all over his face. "Such splendid architecture and workmanship, living proof of how well the missionaries did their job. Their proselytising was a resounding success. It is well over a century later, and the religion of the empire is firmly rooted and flourishing here, as is evident."

"Their proselytising was through the barrel of a gun. How could it not be successful?" I ask tensely.

He gives me a sidelong glance before saying, "The methods employed do not matter. What matters is the outcome, and in that regard the missionary project's success is overwhelming. That you cannot argue with."

"It succeeded by whose standards Cecil? Is success objective or relative?"

He does not respond but instead stamps his foot

again. We are now inside what appears to be a church. It is packed with congregants whose attention is riveted on a man addressing them from a pulpit. There is palpable excitement in the air, an almost feverish atmosphere. It is evident that this church is of the charismatic Pentecostal variety. The man at the pulpit is sharply dressed in a pink designer suit. He preaches in a raised voice that reverberates across the entire building. His voice and words seem to animate the congregation considerably; there is a lot of jumping, shouting and raising of hands from the audience.

"Deuteronomy eighteen verse ten to twelve says, 'Let no one be found among you who is a medium or spiritist or who consults the dead. Anyone who does these things is detestable to the Lord.' Fellow believers, do not be fooled or led astray by those who tell you that communicating with the dead is harmless. They promote these diabolical activities in the name of so-called culture and tradition, but as Christians, our culture is biblical, and our traditions are rooted in the Word of God. The Bible explicitly forbids any form of contact with the deceased, but you find heathens in our society boasting about being guided and led by ancestral spirits. This is nothing more than crude idolatry, replacing the one true God with the spirits of the dead, with evil spirits. It is pitiful and pathetic. It is also dangerous. Grace and salvation can only be found in our risen Lord Jesus Christ, not in worshipping ancestors. Ancestor worship is demonic and a direct gateway to hell! The only spirit we call on is the Holy Spirit, anything else is of the devil! Hallelujah!" the preacher says.

The congregation roars thunderously in approval, and the foundations of the building shake in agreement. I can only look on in consternation.

Turning to me, Cecil says, "Now in your honest opinion, did the missionaries succeed or not?"

"Indoctrinating a people and severing their connection to their spiritual traditions is nothing to be proud of. And we don't worship our ancestors, we honour them and embrace their guidance and protection. They accompany us on our life journeys and we, in turn, are the conduits through which they continue to access and experience the world of the living."

It feels as if something in me has deflated. Another stamp of Cecil's foot, and we find ourselves moving behind a fashionably dressed young woman as she strides purposefully towards an as-yet unknown destination.

"Who is she and why are we following her?" I ask Cecil.

"Let us see where she takes us," comes his vague reply.

I let out an exasperated sigh. We continue shadowing the young woman as she turns into a backstreet on the outskirts of Harare's commercial business district. She enters a dingy shop and exchanges pleasantries with the man and woman behind the counter. She proceeds to ask for a particular brand of skin-lightening lotion which she insists works best for her. I let out a low groan as I watch her receive her purchase. The whole transaction is done matter-of-factly. I glance over at Cecil, and the smug look on his face is annoying to say the least. The young woman thanks the cashiers and leaves. We follow her as she gets into a taxi that leaves her at her place of residence. She enters her abode and deposits her newly-purchased lotion among an assortment of other skin-bleaching creams and products on her dressing table. She appears to be a seasoned collector of them. By the looks of it, she is bordering on becoming a hoarder. Above her dressing table mirror is a picture of white Jesus in a pious pose. I am overcome by dismay.

"Let us step outside," says Cecil, and I oblige.

We stand for a long moment, enveloped by a pregnant silence.

Eventually, I abort the silence. "Eurocentric beauty standards have too many African girls and women in a toxic chokehold. It's disheartening."

"There is nothing toxic to talk of. The young lady we just saw and others like her are merely striving for an ideal, or rather *the* ideal," Cecil says.

"There is absolutely everything wrong with African women distorting and disfiguring themselves because they are striving to attain some false and exclusionary benchmark of beauty. Who says fair skin and European features are the ideal? There is no universal standard of beauty, and there never will be. Beauty is not a monolith, it exists and thrives in multiplicity," I counter.

"From the looks of it, you could benefit from using some of that ointment as well," he says.

"I'm in need of no such ointment. I'm perfectly fine the way I am. More than fine!"

Cecil simply shakes his head. Instead of continuing our back and forth, he stamps his foot once more. We are now standing in an expanse of dusty veld. The landscape is pockmarked with large gaping pits and mounds of sand. I feel as if I have wandered into a no man's land. The atmosphere is unsettling and precarious.

"The eastern part of Rhodesia has always been my favourite," Cecil says, delight etched on his face.

"I take it we're in the Eastern Highlands then. This region certainly has its fair share of breathtaking landscapes, although this place seems to be the exception. Where exactly are we anyway?" I ask, puzzled.

"Where we stand now is an extremely precious place. Don't focus on the outer appearance; the real treasure lies beneath the surface. My blood quickens at the mere thought of it," he says excitedly.

It dawns on me where we are, and why Cecil is filled with enthusiasm all of a sudden.

"Wait a minute…if there's one thing that's synonymous with you, other than shameless pillaging and plundering of vast tracts of Southern Africa, it's diamonds. You were the quintessential colonial diamond mining magnate in your time. And eastern Zimbabwe is known for its massive diamond reserves. I get why you're acting like a kid in a toy store."

"There is nothing I adore more than a diamond. Diamonds are the monarchs of the mineral kingdom; their dazzling beauty and opulence are unmatched. I not only admire these divine gems, I love them. They gave me my fortune and enabled me to do incredible things, unprecedented things. This is hallowed ground. Being in this diamond field feels like being home," Cecil says reverentially.

"As someone who is renowned for forcibly and callously setting up residence in other people's homes, I am not surprised," I quip.

He throws me a withering look, which I promptly return. I look away from him when I begin to feel tremors beneath my feet. The land is shaking noticeably, and I am puzzled as to what might be occurring. As if to answer me, rough diamonds ranging from the size of peas to ostrich eggs start to erupt from the ground and rise into the air as the two of us watch. I look in wonder as they float around us in their hundreds, willing us to reach out and take possession of them. Cecil readily obliges and thirstily plucks a handful out of the air, clutching them to his chest. I tentatively reach out and take one, studying it curiously.

"Diamonds are truly God's gift to mankind. To possess these precious stones is to possess a fountain of wealth," Cecil says. The glee on his face is irritating.

"It's certainly true that diamonds are symbols and generators of wealth. But it's rather unfortunate that in this country, the wealth attached to diamonds only benefits and circulates among an elite few in the ruling class. The proceeds from these diamonds could radically uplift and transform the condition of local communities. We could have state-of-the-art hospitals, excellent schools, beautiful homes, thriving businesses, and the best amenities here. Instead, there is far more impoverishment, lack and hardship than prosperity and progress. The lives of the local people are in a sorry state, even though they are the rightful beneficiaries of this mineral wealth. Why are the masses languishing when their land is so abundantly endowed? Why are foreign corporations seemingly more enriched by this land's natural resources than the populace of the land? It's utterly unjust and a travesty," I say.

"Your diatribe was painful to listen to. What you speak of is not unjust in the least. It is simply the way of nature. The fortunate minority will always prevail over the unfortunate majority, because the minority is stronger and more intellectually advanced, and thus more deserving. They are the thinkers, strategists and masters. The weaker ones will always fall behind the powerful ones. It was such in the nineteenth century, and it remains so in the present. No amount of moralising or hopeless idealism can change this," Cecil tells me.

"That's nothing but social Darwinist hogwash!" I fume.

"Call it what you may, but it is still an indisputable natural law," he calmly says.

I am about to give Cecil a scathing reply when he stamps his foot yet again. We are now standing on a well-manicured lawn in front of a picturesque building. The sign at its entrance reads 'The Boutique Hotel'.

"It feels absolutely delightful to be back in Nyanga again. This was my holiday home when I was still a mortal. They converted it into a hotel some years after my death," Cecil says, pleasant nostalgia animating his voice.

"Let us go inside for some tea," Cecil says cordially. We walk up the front steps and enter the hotel. He leads me to the restaurant and sits at a table. I follow suit. The staff and other restaurant patrons are blissfully unaware of our presence.

Once seated, I notice the tea set at our table is made of stone. I stare at it for a long moment.

"This tea set is made from raw granite?" I ask Cecil.

"Correct. Lovely, isn't it?"

"Interesting," I say.

He takes the granite teapot and pours tea, first into his cup, and then mine.

"I presume you take your tea without milk," says Cecil sardonically.

"Correct. And I presume you take yours drenched in so much milk it overpowers the actual flavour of the tea," I retort.

We sit silently, sipping from our stone teacups and lost in our individual musings. The silence is abruptly shattered by a piercing wail. I sense a deep anguish and despair in the sound. It is so jarring, I jump in my chair. The wail is joined by another one, then another, until a choir of them are assailing us.

"What on earth is that ghastly noise? I can hardly drink my tea properly," Cecil states in annoyance.

I am about to respond that I have no idea what the noise is, when I glance outside the large window next to us and inhale sharply. Headed steadily in our direction are a horde of skeletons – the disconcerting wails are coming from them. They are striding purposefully in unison. I turn to Cecil to ask if he is seeing what I am seeing. The look on his ashen face gives me my answer.

"What in the bloody hell is this?" Cecil whispers.

We both instinctively get up from the table and head for the hotel entrance where we stand and watch. The skeletons stop just shy of the steps leading up to the entrance. Their wailing is now interspersed with odd shrieks and shouts. They begin to chant, and at first, I cannot make out what they are saying, but I gradually pick up that they are chanting in Shona.

"*Dzosa nhaka yedu, dzosa zvese zvawakatora*!" they chant rhythmically.

"They are saying 'give us back our inheritance, give us back everything you took'. I have a feeling their grievance is directed at you," I tell Cecil.

He snorts. "It is entirely their fault if I managed to take possession of what they *think* is theirs. The blame lies squarely with them for not being able to defend their property, tangible or intangible."

"You are such a stereotypical coloniser, completely remorseless," I say in disgust.

"I believe I am rather the archetypal coloniser and quite proud of it," is his imperious response.

"Your basic wordplay doesn't sanitise your lack of a moral conscience."

Cecil shrugs. He proceeds to square his shoulders and face the agitated skeletons. I wonder what will transpire. He addresses the skeletons in a contemptuous voice.

"Can you heap of bones please take your ruckus elsewhere? Any grievances you may have had with me should have been addressed when we were all alive. It's rather pointless now, I think. Now bugger off and let me drink my tea in peace."

The skeletons are quiet while he speaks, listening, but as soon as he finishes, they resume their melody of wailing, shrieking and chanting. But there is a change in their tone this time, an ominous one. They sound more guttural and, whereas earlier they had sounded aggrieved, they now seem menacing. Their skulls begin to contort and twist grotesquely. The atmosphere darkens around us. Cecil has stoked a smouldering fire.

"They don't seem so happy. I think you should have addressed them in a more courteous manner. Can you handle their wrath, Cecil?" I ask jovially.

At this point, their wails are more of battle cries. I watch in amazement as blood begins to ooze from their bony frames. At that same moment, blood begins to drip from Cecil's palms. I look from the blood-drenched skeletons to Cecil and back again. The sight of the blood makes me feel like a thousand insects are crawling all over my skin. I shiver despite myself. The skeletons begin to slowly advance up the steps. Their intent is evidently far from innocuous. I am not alarmed in the least because I know I am not their target. I look over at Cecil and see that he is breathing hard. I chuckle to myself.

"I believe our time here is done. We can visit again when it is more conducive and finish drinking our tea then," Cecil says, with a slight tremor in his voice.

"A little scared of the bones of the past are you?" I

ask in amusement.

Cecil's eyes are trained on the approaching skeletons as he stamps his foot vigorously. We are teleported back to Harare's central business district. We are now standing before the statue of Mbuya Nehanda, the famed nineteenth century Shona spirit medium and anti-colonial heroine. Cecil's palms are no longer soaked in blood. As I gaze at Mbuya Nehanda's bronze figure, reminiscent of sacred African femininity at its most defiant, I hear a lioness roaring in the vicinity. I look around but see nothing. It slowly dawns on me that the roar came from the statue itself.

"She was an absolutely remarkable person. Her bravery during the First Chimurenga uprising is highly inspiring, and her legacy is enduring," I comment, still gazing at the statue.

"My men called her 'the great witch of Mashonaland'. As one of the leaders of the 1896 native revolt, she was a formidable opponent, I will grant her that. She had unusual courage for a female. Of course, none of that matters; she was ultimately captured and executed," Cecil says.

"Courage is a human trait; it is neither masculine nor feminine. You may have succeeded in executing her, but you failed to break her spirit. She remained unbowed to the end. Her famous words as she was about to be hanged, when she said her bones would rise again, are testament to that. You saw the skeletons back there, did you not?" I say.

"Nonsense. Those delusional remains need to return to whatever dismal abyss they crawled out of. I'm quite annoyed at how they interrupted a perfectly pleasant tea ceremony," Cecil huffs.

"You seemed more shaken than annoyed from my recollection," I say, with a smirk.

Before he can respond, our attention is drawn to loud noises coming from nearby. I look to see what is going on. There is a mass of people moving up the street, singing and chanting slogans as they move. Some of them are *toyi-toying* and waving placards militantly. Their frustration and fury are palpable.

"This type of anarchy is unacceptable. It needlessly upsets the social fabric," says Cecil disapprovingly.

"This is hardly anarchy. It's just ordinary people actively expressing their discontent, as they rightfully should."

"They can express their discontent civilly and respectfully," Cecil retorts.

"When one is deprived of authority or decision-making power, sometimes demonstrating in this manner is the only way for one to assert agency," I explain.

Cecil frowns. As the demonstrators pass us, several

police trucks suddenly appear ahead of them. My heart sinks. It is the dreaded riot police. I watch as they launch out of the trucks with their helmets and heavy boots. I know what will happen next. I watch in horror as batons strike skin and bone, boots kick vulnerable flesh, teargas blankets the atmosphere and rubber bullets tear into bodies already softened by suffering. Screams, tears, and blood mingle on the sunny Harare day. The once-defiant protesters tumble like fallen heroes, collapsing under the weight of a seemingly impenetrable system, capitulating to official ruthlessness. The sledgehammer of repression is pounding them into submission, their grievances completely irrelevant to the powers-that-be. They are now broken shards of glass, and my heart bleeds for their lot. This is what it means to be a subaltern, deprived of even the smallest morsel of compassion, profoundly dehumanised.

As I take in this heartbreaking scene, two dozen uniformed white men on horses appear out of thin air. While I am trying to figure out who these newcomers could be, they start viciously assaulting the protesters alongside the riot police. It is apparent they are working in tandem with the riot police to violently suppress and disperse the protesters. From what I can see, the mounted men are more brutal than their counterparts. The defenceless protesters stand no chance against the lethal combined forces of the riot police and the men on horses.

"Who are those guys on horseback and why are they making an already horrible situation worse?" I ask.

"Those are my men. Glad to see them discharging their duties diligently and stamping out anarchy. Insurrection must never be allowed to take root. It must be snuffed out as soon as it rears its treasonous head," Cecil answers me.

"What do you mean when you say those are your men?" I ask nervously.

"The British South Africa Police."

I shake my head in astonishment. The men on horses are ghosts of the Rhodesian police. How eerie. But it is not surprising, since the local police force itself is a colonial invention and relic. The phantoms of Rhodesian police showing up in this instance makes perfect sense, since they are the forebears of this generation's much-feared riot police. Violence born from violence. Injustice born from injustice. Cycles in a continuum. And it is the masses of the land who pay the highest price, from the late nineteenth century to the present day. Cecil's words echo in my mind hauntingly: "Rhodesia will never die. Rhodesia is very much alive now, as it was before."

Hot tears well up from my depths and sting my eyes as they cascade down my cheeks. A one hundred and thirty five year old rage rises in me and grips every fibre of my being. It is in that moment that I resolve to kill Rhodesia, to strangle and suffocate it the way it has done my people's spirits, until it expires permanently. Rhodesia must die. Even if it kills me in the process. Killing Rhodesia is the only way to stop it reproducing itself in my society and mutating in the minds of my people once and for all. In that moment, Tateguru and Muchembere's faces appear before me. Their expressions are solemn. Just as suddenly, they disappear without saying a word.

Cecil is looking at me oddly. "It is folly to think you can challenge a behemoth and come out victorious…or even alive. The spirit of the empire is too deeply rooted. It cannot be exorcised and it would be pointless to try," he says. There is a threatening edge to his voice.

The temperature seems to drop by multiple degrees, and I shiver involuntarily.

"Nothing in this world is invincible Cecil. We both know the once-mighty British Empire dissolved in the latter half of the twentieth century. The empire fell, so why should I fear to confront its remnants?" I ask with a steady voice, even though my heart is pounding.

"Indeed, the great British Empire may have fallen in a territorial sense, which was of course a regrettable loss. But even though the colonies may have slipped away, the empire still reigns in the minds, perceptions, attitudes and beliefs of millions upon millions. Subliminally, it remains supreme and triumphant. Its influence and power are embedded on the deeper mental plane, on the intangible spectrum of existence, and it shall continue this way for infinity. It is impossible to uproot," Cecil declares.

"Impossible according to who? I assure you the

empire is definitely falling in the minds of many as we speak. These are different times we are living in; the winds of reclamation and restoration are blowing strongly. The once colonised are reclaiming their truth in unprecedented ways. Your glory days of imperial exceptionalism are over and done; the sooner you accept this the better," I tell him.

3

As soon as I finish speaking, the irises of Cecil's eyes turn a bright orange. I am caught off guard and I take an involuntary step backward. I am reminded of the venomous orange eyes of the shape-shifting entity that appeared to me the other night. Cecil is visibly infuriated; I have clearly struck a nerve. I tell myself not to succumb to fear and face his anger squarely. I remind myself that in my lineage, we are described as having hearts of stone, we are made of warrior stock. I draw on those reserves and steel myself for whatever may ensue.

His eyes flash as he says, "You speak heresy. The spirit of the empire is far too vast and powerful to lose its relevance. Your views are as insignificant as you are."

He is increasing in size with each word. I watch in amazement as he steadily grows larger and larger. In no time, he dwarfs the city buildings, and my neck starts hurting from craning to look up at his ever-growing frame. As I am engrossed in watching Cecil expand, a heavy gust of wind appears and whips me so strongly that I stagger a bit. Instead of passing and continuing on its way, the wave of wind lingers and encircles me. I can feel its pressure bearing on me from all sides. And then I am being lifted up. The wind seems to have grown invisible hands that are carrying me up and up. It takes me a moment to realise that I am in the middle of a whirlwind that is transporting me towards the heavens. I have no idea where I am being taken, but I surrender to the experience. I have no choice either way. I feel weightless. I imagine myself ending up in outer space, drifting among the multiple moons of Saturn.

Just as I am relaxing into this upliftment, it abruptly stops. I expect to tumble unceremoniously to the ground and shatter fatally, but instead, I find myself floating comfortably above the clouds.

"Glad you can join me in the heights," a voice says, startling me.

It is Cecil. I am hovering slightly above his impossibly gigantic frame. The scale of him is immense, his enormity mind-boggling. From this vantage point, I can see his legs stretched out across a wide teapot-shaped distance. His gargantuan legs are straddling Zimbabwe – one foot is positioned on the banks of the Zambezi River in the north, and the other is just shy of the Limpopo River in the south. I am reminded of the popular Rhodes Colossus cartoon that depicted a giant Cecil looming over Africa with arms outstretched, one leg in the Cape to the south, the other in Cairo to the north. His body overshadows the length and breadth of the land. He is surveying Zimbabwe as if it is his private property still, as if he is lord of this land that I call home. This makes my blood boil. How dare he act like he owns this house of stone that he invaded and renovated in ways that remain highly detrimental to its inhabitants?

I watch in consternation as puppet strings sprout from Cecil's fingers. They dangle in the air pointedly before moving to attach themselves to the vast majority of the people of Zimbabwe. Only a very small percentage of them are exempt. I continue watching as he moves the masses this way and the leadership that way, like marionettes. He is pulling the strings of business and industry, schools and universities, churches, households, the electoral system, the elites. There is no resistance because there is no conscious awareness. He is in full control, and the people are at the mercy of his whims. There is neither authentic autonomy nor practical independence. It is all a charade.

"What use is physical sovereignty when the mind remains captured?" I ask no one in particular. "Why are we not waking up? Why can't we see that we are still chained and yoked, that liberation was only won on the surface? Why are we not cutting these strings and setting fire to the feet of the puppet master?"

"You can shout into the void all you want; it won't change anything. You may have taken the land, but I still run the show, I still exert massive control. You may have the soil, but the Rhodesian spirit still dominates. This is irrefutable," says Cecil coldly.

"You don't run anything Cecil. You're just a stubborn colonial demon, clinging to memories of past conquests and refusing to be cast out. It's pathetic. It's time for you to set this land free. It doesn't belong to you, and it never did," I say in a measured tone.

"Shut up you stupid kaffir wench! You know

nothing! I am growing tired of your nonsense!" he yells.

On hearing the phrase "stupid kaffir wench", a very ancient fury explodes within me. The time for civility is clearly over, and I have never had a problem adjusting to changed circumstances.

"What did you call me? Apologise now," I say calmly but firmly.

"I will do no such thing. You have become an annoyance. A stupid kaffir wench is exactly what you are!"

"So, you actually repeated it?" I pause. "I assure you, you have just made the greatest mistake of your dead life. Now you must be humbled."

He lets out a scornful chuckle. I silently call for ancestral assistance, and I am almost immediately answered when Tateguru appears in front of me, holding out my staff. I thank him as I take it from his hand before he vanishes back into the ether.

I turn to Cecil. "I have entertained you all this while, even after all the unforgivable things you have done to this land and its people, the land of my foremothers and forefathers, the land in whose soil my umbilical cord is buried. I should have known better. But now you have crossed the line, and for that you will atone. What I am about to do is not just for me, it is also retribution for my ancestors. I am enacting vengeance on their behalf, because their justice is equally mine as well. The first thing I am going to do is reclaim something you stole from my people, something that's rightfully ours. Today it returns to its owners."

I feel possessed by a mighty force and a primordial power.

"What can your puny self do to me? Absolutely nothing," Cecil says mockingly.

"Is that so? Well, my puny self can start by making your overconfident self just as puny as I am."

I point my staff at his forehead as ancient Karanga incantations rise in my throat and pour out of my mouth. I have no idea how I am able to speak this language of old, the precursor to modern Shona, but I am not very surprised. It is the original form of my mother tongue after all, my first language, embedded in my genes. As I am incantating, the whirlwind transforms from a benign phenomenon to a ferocious dark storm. My words are seemingly imbued with the power to influence the elements and I find this quite fascinating. I have never felt more lucid and focused.

Cecil is looking around uncertainly, his earlier self-assurance gone. He begins to gradually reduce in size. I keep my staff steadily aimed at him as I continue to pelt him with ancient words. He starts flailing around desperately and shouting in dismay, but I hold steady. I only stop when he has been reduced to normal size. The storm quiets itself and reverts to a whirlwind which deposits me back on the ground, next to Cecil. He looks extremely disoriented. A strong sense of satisfaction cascades over me, but this feeling lasts only briefly as I am overcome by an overwhelming sense of urgency.

"Now that you and I are on an equal footing, we have unfinished business. You have something of mine that you must return. A very precious and cherished historical emblem that you stole from the ancient stone city of Great Zimbabwe. It is of great spiritual significance to my people, yet you took it and shamelessly appropriated it. I'm sure you know what I'm referring to."

Cecil's face takes on a contemptuous expression. "Do not delude yourself into thinking you have any actual power over me, or that you can order me around. Your little trick that you just pulled was nothing special. In fact, I allowed you to do that so you could feel what it is like to have some kind of victory, but I assure you that I will not let it happen again. You are no match for me. All I have to do is unleash my forces on you and you will be vanquished. As for your request, I am well aware of what you refer to. But I will not be returning anything to you or any of your ilk. It is now mine! I am not answerable to you. I will not be handing anything in my possession over to your inconsequential person. End of story." His eyes take on the orange glow once again.

I raise my eyebrows. "So, you will not willingly give it back?"

He shakes his head and crosses his arms over his chest.

"That's perfectly fine. I will have to take it against your will then," I inform him.

"Try it. You will fail dismally."

I nod my head as a sign of accepting the challenge, before pointing my staff at the horizon and saying, "To Cape Town."

We are instantaneously transported to an estate in Cape Town, in the neighbouring country of South Africa. I make my way towards an old white mansion that is the cornerstone of the estate, with Cecil trotting next to me. There is no sign of human presence or activity, other than myself. Without being told, I understand that I have entered another parallel world adjacent to the one I was just in. This one has a different essence. It feels like a rarefied battleground, one which requires no distractions or encroachments from the ordinary world.

As I am walking, a bird flies close above me and I stop to study it. I recognise the bird intuitively. It is a *chapungu*, the rare bateleur eagle. It is considered highly sacred by my people and, more importantly, represents what I am here to collect – the stone-carved bird sculpture that was stolen by white settlers from Great Zimbabwe in the nineteenth century before being passed on to Cecil Rhodes. It is one of eight soapstone bird sculptures that were looted and ended up outside Zimbabwe, but almost all of them have since returned home, except this one that remains in Cape Town. These stone avian sculptures, commonly called the Zimbabwe Birds, are greatly revered in Zimbabwe, and the continued absence of one of them has created an imbalance in the spiritual and cultural ecosystem of the land. The return of this bird is long overdue, and today I will ensure it finally flies back home.

The mansion I am headed for was Cecil's residence during his living years. I am not here for sightseeing or a historical tour; I am here to reclaim what is mine. That which belongs to my people is imprisoned in Cecil's former home, and I am determined to free it at all costs. As I approach the house-cum-prison, I am greeted by a sight that stops me in my tracks. Four rows of the ghost British South Africa Police are stationed in front of the house, rifles cocked, waiting for me with expressionless faces. There are about a dozen in each row, and they are not on horseback, unlike earlier. I was not expecting this in the least, but I tell myself to remain calm.

"I told you not to attempt this doomed mission of yours. You will never be a match for me. You can turn back now, concede defeat, and save yourself. Or you can foolishly continue if you are suicidal," Cecil says.

"One thing you will soon learn about me is that 'defeat' is never an option," I retort, my eyes riveted on the ghost policemen ahead of me.

"Your defiance will be your destruction," says Cecil

icily.

"Quite the contrary; it will be yours Cecil."

I go on my knees and begin to clap rhythmically. I invoke the protection and assistance of my ancestors as I have done numerous times before. But now I need their intervention more than ever. This is a critical time; a great deal is at stake, and I have never felt more on edge. The odds are not in my favour, and my ancestors are the only ones I can rely on as my comrades-in-arms. In no time, Tateguru and Muchembere appear in front of me and I feel instantly strengthened. Tateguru hands me a *bakatwa* and a *pfumo*. I take the double-edged sword and spear without hesitation.

"No harm will befall you. Do what is necessary to accomplish your mission," Muchembere says. I nod my head and thank them before they disappear.

I take a deep breath, stand up, and face the ghost police squad. Then I begin to walk towards them. There is a surprising equanimity within me – I feel neither fear nor confidence. I am in that perfect middle space, and I am ready for anything. The ghost colonial police take aim, but I do not stop advancing.

I hear Cecil speak from somewhere behind me, "Your performance of bravery is interesting to behold, but this is the time for you to surrender and retreat. My men will send you to the lowest depths of Hades without a second thought. If you stop now, I will allow you to go back to your child and resume your life, unharmed. If you continue, you will have chosen your damnation."

The mention of Ruva almost makes me stop and turn around. Tears fill my eyes as an image of my beloved daughter appears in my mind's eye. The thought of potentially not returning to her is gut-wrenching, but I am now at the service of something far greater than myself; I must soldier on and pray to emerge out of this ordeal intact. I keep advancing.

Cecil shouts, "Annihilate her!" The ghost policemen all pull their triggers. Everything seems to slow down. I watch a multitude of fiery bullets flying toward me. I do not feel panic or dread. If my blood is meant to be spilled in the pursuit of this mission, then so be it. I am prepared for any eventuality.

Just then, a figure clad in a hooded grey robe starts walking next to me. I peer to see who it is, but in the space where their face should be there is... nothing, only an impossible darkness. The figure is holding a scythe, and it dawns on me that I am walking with the Grim Reaper. On my other side, I see Tateguru walking in step with me. I have Death on my left, and Continuity of Life on my right. Equilibrium personified.

The fire bullets have almost reached me. I prepare myself for the impact and the fateful moment of elimination. Then something strange happens. The bullets suddenly come to a halt in mid-air, just before striking me.

I look at them suspended in air, their miniature flames dancing maliciously. Then I watch in disbelief as they start liquefying and falling to the ground harmlessly. The ghost police fire again, but the same thing happens – their bullets of fire again transform into water. It happens again and again. Their ammunition is being neutralised by some unknown force. I am fascinated and immensely relieved. I look to my left. The Grim Reaper is not there anymore, but Tateguru is still on my right. I look over at Cecil. The look of utter perplexity on his face almost makes me chuckle. The ghost Rhodesian policemen have stopped firing and are now standing around helplessly.

Tateguru puts his hand on my shoulder and says, "Make your lineage proud."

On hearing these words, it is as if a higher energy enters my body and takes over, propelling me towards the ghost policemen. Today they will die anew, death on top of death. My determination is ironclad. As I reach the phantom colonial police, I see the Grim Reaper positioned next to them and I am energised even more. I raise the *pfumo* and *bakatwa* and begin stabbing, cutting, slicing and striking with deadly precision. It is as if I am possessed by some preternatural force; I have no idea how I am wielding these weapons so lethally. All around me, spectral bodies are falling one after the other. Trying to kill me was a grave mistake on their part. I mow them down mercilessly, and I do not stop until all of them are vanquished.

When I am finally done, I am breathless with

exertion. A large metal door appears next to the Grim Reaper and swings open. Inside it, I see what looks like a desolate wasteland from which blood-curdling shrieks and eerie howls emanate. One by one, the fallen Rhodesian policemen are sucked into the open door, and the Grim Reaper follows them inside before the door closes and vanishes as mysteriously as it appeared, swallowed phantoms and all. I take a moment to catch my breath and then turn to Cecil.

"I told you defeat is not an option for me. The nightmare is only beginning for you. I will deal with you later; for now, I go to reclaim stolen property."

"You have no right to take any of my possessions. That is outright theft," Cecil says bitterly.

"How ironic. You can gaslight me all you want, I'm still taking back what's rightfully mine," I say. I head for the short flight of steps leading to the front door of the mansion. Cecil scurries after me.

I enter the house and head for Cecil's old bedroom where the Zimbabwe Bird is kept in captivity. Although I have never been in this residence before, I navigate the space with ease, my inner compass leading me with accuracy. There are carved likenesses of the Zimbabwe Bird incorporated into the wooden staircase and designed into doorplates in the house. There is an obvious fixation with the sacred bird of my people. I stop to stare at the huge granite bathtub in the main bathroom, before finally entering Cecil's old bedroom. The room feels extraordinarily chilly. It is as if I have walked into a freezer.

I look around and my eyes fall on an antique glass display case near the bed and I walk over to it. The display case contains what appear to be souvenirs. What I have come for is on the top shelf. On laying eyes on the Zimbabwe Bird, I am overcome by a wave of awe and wonder. I feel like kneeling before the bird and reciting elaborate praise poetry. The story of a nation is written in its form – all the triumphs, losses, creativity, blessings, subjugation, heritage, struggles, politics, prosperity, and potential. The heights and falls of a land. The dreams and efforts of a people. The disappointments experienced and the glories still to come. The sheer resilience and forging on. The refusal to collapse completely. The continuous rebuilding. The resourcefulness and industriousness. The ability to laugh in the face of failure and rise once more. This exalted bird represents a journey that has been rich, profound, bruising, uncertain and still ongoing. Reverence is the only offering befitting its stature and significance, and that is what I give it.

"Leave it alone! Do not dare touch it!" Cecil hisses nearby.

I ignore him. A golden key materialises just above me. I reach out, take the key, and unlock the display case with trembling hands. As I open the case door, it feels as if the weight of the entire universe is bearing down on me. Cecil is making strange, tortured sounds somewhere close by, but I pay him no heed. I am too overwhelmed by being face to face with a national treasure. I feel unqualified to handle this priceless artefact, but I am duty-bound to do so. I reach for the bird and hesitate a little before touching it. On making contact with it, I feel a powerful surge course through me, and I pull my hand back sharply. I wait for a short while before slowly reaching for the bird again, and this time no unexpected sensation occurs.

I take it out of the display case and hold it carefully. Cecil lets out a strangled cry. He tries to lunge for the bird, but an invisible force repels him, and he stumbles unceremoniously to the floor.

I address the hallowed stone bird. "You have been held captive for too long. Today you are liberated from your cage. You are free to return home to the house of stone and bring desperately needed completion. Your land awaits you."

I carry it carefully out of the room and outside the house, Cecil behind me. The bird rises from my hands and spreads its stone wings majestically. It transfigures and doubles in size into an actual *chapungu*, the sacred messenger bird of the High God, Mwari, and the ancestors. It flaps its wings powerfully and takes flight without looking back. Cecil bellows in despair while I let out a great shout of joy. A grave wrong has finally been righted. The scales of justice tip close to the point of perfect balance. Not quite, but almost there.

I tell my *tsvimbo* that I want to follow the great

bird. In an instant, I find myself encompassed by monumental dry stone walls and an air of timeless splendour. I cannot help but marvel at the beauty of the masonry on display around me, at the ingenuity of the well-shaped granite blocks perfectly stacked with no mortar to bind them. I am back on home soil, in the Great Enclosure of the ancient city of Great Zimbabwe. I am dwarfed by the massive scale of this structure I am in, and I almost feel compelled to pay tribute to its magnificence. The knowledge that my ancestors built this unparalleled edifice fills me with an overflow of pride and gratitude. I am the descendant of supreme skill, imagination, and craftsmanship.

But I am not the only one awed by Great Zimbabwe's beauty. Next to me Cecil exclaims, "King Solomon's famed mines! Still as glorious as they were over a century ago when I first laid eyes on them!"

I am starting to think we are possibly conjoined. He is always there.

I grimace. "You can't possibly still believe that outdated and outlandish theory of Great Zimbabwe being King Solomon's mines! It was disproved aeons ago. Listen here, Cecil, Great Zimbabwe was constructed by the VaKaranga and it was a Karanga city. It's not some biblical legend. Let go of false narratives and accept the truth."

"Impossible! No native could have built anything this brilliant. Never! That is nothing but pure fabrication,"

Cecil says vehemently.

"You clearly can't stomach the thought of my people being exceptionally gifted and creative, and that's quite pathetic. You can remain in denial all you want, but my forebears constructed this. Whether you agree or not makes no difference whatsoever. This is my cultural heritage we are admiring. End of story."

A haunting female voice begins to sing in the vicinity, startling us both. It is singing the traditional folk song 'Mudzimu Dzoka' which implores a legendary ancestor to return. The voice is so painstakingly sublime that I feel goosebumps on my skin. This is what ethereal sounds like. As I listen to the song, I am overcome by an intense nostalgia for a life lived many, many years before this one. Something compels me to look behind, and when I do, I am shocked to see myself – a mirror me. Her features are exactly like mine, down to the beauty mark on her nose. But unlike me, her hair is short, and she is wrapped in a single piece of flowing black cloth. She is barefoot and radiant. There is such a depth of purity in her eyes that I feel unworthy to be in her presence. I am too tarnished by traumas small and large, too afflicted by the maladies of modernity. Too much of an existential misfit. I am disconnected from the original core of self, the very heart of being. How can she look at me with such understanding and lack of judgement? How can she radiate such love and loyalty? Who told her I was deserving?

She beckons me to come closer. I hesitate, but I feel

myself somehow automatically moving towards her. I am unable to resist her even if I desperately wanted to. When I reach her, she extends her hand, and I stare at it for what feels like an infinity. Eventually I lift my own tentatively and place it in hers. I am instantly consumed by a sense of wholeness so potent that I almost stagger. I can feel Mirror Me transmitting waves of unconditional and everlasting companionship to my broken being. Repairing me. Cleaning and bandaging wounds. Sterilising the bacteria. Treating the root causes. Cutting away the gangrene. Dusting away the confusion. Sweeping and polishing the floors of my being. Restoration. Back to the moment of creation, the first point of existence. Unpolluted. Uncorrupted. Unlimited. Blindingly blessed. Me as I truly am, not as I have been influenced or conditioned to be. Panoramic. Vast. Borderless. Complete.

I break down in wracking sobs. Weights and loads fall off my body and drop to the ground – all shapes, sizes, and depths of them. With each agonising sob, I feel lighter. Mirror Me pulls me into an embrace that feels like lying down to rest after a lengthy, exhausting journey. She and I seem to merge into one another. The wall of separation has fallen. The cold war between my mortal self and spirit has come to an end. Reunification. I hear thunderous applause from an unseen source. Generations of my lineage are cheering and applauding me for allowing the medicine to enter and work its therapeutic power. This is not only a gift to myself, but to those before and after me. The effect is communal. My healing gives them wings as well. *Unhu* actualised.

I hear that transcendent singing voice once again and its mystical song. It is invoking and awakening. I wonder if it is Mirror Me singing. Or is it me? Without being told, I know it is both of us singing. The voice is coming from our most ancient part, from the roots of our baobab tree.

"Look up there," Mirror Me says telepathically from within me.

I look up and see eight forms descending from the sky. The stone Zimbabwe Birds reunited and complete, the family unit intact once more. The sight makes me so ecstatic, I let out a joyous laugh. Eight columns appear in a circular formation on the ground, the columns the sculptures originally stood on aeons ago. I watch as the birds descend and sit on their thrones, absorbing the momentous scene reverently, feeling immensely humbled to witness such a historic happening. Muchembere and Tateguru appear next to me.

"Well done my child. You have faced fear and adversity with admirable grace and fulfilled an extraordinary task. The land is grateful. Those in the heavens are celebrating you. And now you receive your just reward," Muchembere says proudly. Tateguru is grinning at me.

I am wondering what reward I could possibly receive, when the deafening sound of an elephant's trumpet rings out and shakes the whole area. I clutch Muchembere's arm in panic, but she only pats my hand reassuringly. As I am gathering myself, an immense elephant materialises in front of us. Sitting atop it is quite possibly the most wondrous man I have ever seen. He has silver-grey dreadlocks cascading down to his waist, and he is draped in a fine leopard skin. Gold jewellery decorates his neck and hands, and a *ndoro* conus shell disc adorns his forehead. A dazzling white spear is floating next to him. He is enveloped by a light of such brilliance, it defies comprehension, and the power emanating from him is remarkable. I have never experienced such might coming from any being. His regal face has a warm expression as he looks down at us. Tateguru and Muchembere kneel before him and I follow suit.

"Who is he?" I ask in a whisper.

"He is the great Murenga Pfumojena Sororenzou, the founding father and original king of the Shona people. He is not only our founding ancestor, he is also a revered deity who wields immeasurable authority in our land. The two Chimurenga liberation wars against colonial rule were fought in his name. To be in his presence in this way is an extraordinary honour that very few are privileged to have," Tateguru answers in a low voice.

I am awestruck. I have read and heard about the legendary Murenga and his highly venerated place in Shona culture and history. To have him in front of me is surreal. Instead of keeping my gaze lowered respectfully, I stare at him in open-mouthed wonderment. When he starts addressing me, it feels as if I could just faint.

"MaMoyo, you have proved yourself worthy of the role we chose for you. We worried that you might struggle to accomplish your assignment, but you have laid those worries to rest. You have made us proud and healed a deep wound by helping to bring back our sacred and cherished bird, something which was long overdue. Now come and receive what is yours," Murenga says in a mesmeric voice.

I look at both Muchembere and Tateguru nervously and they both nod to me. I get up from my knees and stand before our god-king. He smiles at me as he takes hold of his white spear and points it at me. My upper body is instantly attired in a lion skin traditional apron, and a sceptre appears in my right hand. It is of high quality wood and is studded along the entirety of its length with luminous gold pieces, with its head carved into the representation of a human heart. A *ndoro* disc positions itself in the centre of my forehead, held in place by a thin black band that encircles my head.

"You have attained the position of *mhondoro yenyika*, the most elevated spirit medium of the land. You are no longer just *svikiro redzinza*, the spiritual vessel for your clan only. You now protect and take care of the whole of this territory now called Zimbabwe, but which I know as Chivavarira, the sacred promised land. From this moment on, your heart beats in unison with the heartbeat of this land. This means you are now vested with far greater powers, and with that, greater responsibility. A great deal more will be required and asked of you going forward. In your new role, you have one more pressing task left to complete – a mission pertaining to the colonising spirit that ruthlessly invaded, destabilised and desecrated our land. I am sure you know what task I am referring to," says Murenga.

"I am beyond grateful for this great honour you have bestowed on me, my king. I am not entirely sure if I am deserving of it, but I humbly accept with a thankful heart. And yes, I am aware of the remaining task you talk of. I am ready to carry it out and fulfil the mission," I say.

"You are extremely deserving and very worthy, my daughter, you should never doubt that. You are a shining star and the apple of Nyikadzimu, the ancestral realm. Go forth and continue to make us proud. We are counting on you." Another earth-shattering trumpet from the elephant and both the animal and Murenga vanish out of sight.

I remain standing there, trying to process the significance of what has just transpired and its effect on me. I involuntarily shake my head in disbelief. I cannot help wishing Mother and Ruva were here to witness it with me. I know life will never be the same again, and this both excites me and makes me nervous. Muchembere walks up to me and puts her arm around my shoulders, as if to encourage and strengthen me for the unknown road ahead.

"You were born for this, my dearest child. This is your life's purpose and you will excel at it, as you have at everything else you have done," she says confidently.

I feel the same way I did as a little girl when I faced something new and intimidating – deeply anxious yet also eager to triumph. I suddenly experience a strong urge to curl up in foetal position and withdraw into my cocoon but that is not a possibility.

I turn to Muchembere. "With guidance from you and Tateguru, and the rest of Nyikadzimu supporting me, I know I will make it. The knowledge that I have a benevolent multitude journeying and fighting alongside me is empowering, and it gives me the confidence to take up this mantle. I cannot lose when I am backed by such a highly sacred community everywhere I am."

Muchembere ululates joyfully, and I once again hear disembodied applause and cheers. I allow myself to bask in the moment. For the first time since I was eleven, I truly feel gifted and not cursed. I can now revel in the parts of myself I used to loathe and resent, finally. I recall the encounter with the *mupositori* all those years ago and what he said about me. I cannot help grinning with delight.

Cecil's acidic voice interrupts my newfound bliss. "All this empty pomp and gratuitous sentimentality is revolting, and it amounts to nothing! I created this country, and I still own it. It belongs to me! There is nothing you inferior lot can do to change that. Not now, not in a thousand years!"

I slowly turn to him. "Not in a thousand years, you say? The last time a white Rhodesian said something similar, he was roundly humiliated, so we'll see about that. It appears we have reached the culmination of our interaction. I can't say my time with you was pleasant, but it was certainly informative. Now let's finish what you started back in 1890. Today what you wrongfully took from us and falsely claimed as yours is being restored. I am taking back what's ours from your thieving, plundering hands. Your inglorious reign has come to its bitter end," I say coldly.

Cecil lets out a maniacal hyena laugh. His eyes turn completely orange and his appearance becomes ghoulish. His true form is presenting itself in all its distastefulness.

"The only thing coming to an end is you, idiotic girl. I told you before that you are no match for me. I am an empire-builder, a man of fortune and greatness. I am unprecedented and unconquerable. Someone of your kind is microscopic to me, no threat at all."

"You really need to stop calling me names, Cecil. You must know by now it doesn't end well for you when you do that," I say in exasperation.

"I will call you whatever I damn well please."

I realise that continuing to talk to him is futile, so I stamp my sceptre on the ground. We are instantly transported to a rocky hill overlooking an alluringly scenic valley terrain. The hill is part of a network of granite hills naturally fashioned into enigmatic shapes and designs. Standing here, I feel as stable and harmonious as the balancing boulders in my vicinity. This is Matobo Hills and it is an extremely sacred landscape. It has been a shrine, pilgrimage site, and spiritual centre for hundreds of years. It is the place where we commune with Mwari, the High God, and petition the spirit realm for rain. The hill we are standing on is known as Malindadzimu, the resting place of the benevolent spirits. The presence of departed ones is always palpable here; it is a place where the line between the spirit world and the world of the living is blurred, there is no clear demarcation.

"I see you decided to bring me home to the View of the World," Cecil says, calling Malindadzimu by the name he christened it while he was still alive.

He saunters to a nearby grave cut into the hill. There is a brass plaque on top of this granite tomb which reads "Here lie the remains of Cecil John Rhodes." Before his death, Cecil instructed that he wished to be interred on Malindadzimu when he died. He proceeds to sit on top of his grave, facing me.

"As if ransacking this land and subjugating its people wasn't enough, you also had to defile our sacred shrine with your sordid remains. The height of disrespect!" I yell furiously.

He glares daggers at me. "I am the supreme spirit of the land now. All your little ancestral spirits bow before me. I am the ruler and conqueror in death, just as I was while alive. And there is absolutely nothing you can do about it."

"Is that so? I'm always energised by a good challenge. It seems we have come to the time of exorcism. You and

Rhodesia are about to experience your final eviction! Your time is up Cecil. Pack your settler colonial baggage and leave our land. If you won't go voluntarily, then I will have to make you leave!" My warning is resolute.

Cecil leaps up, his face twisted in fury. "You dare to attempt to dethrone me? You have the gall to think you can send me packing? You are out of your mind! I have dealt with your foolishness long enough. I blessed you with the honour of being in my presence and engaging with me, even though you were utterly undeserving. And instead of being grateful, you keep inundating me with consistent rubbish. Enough! My patience has run out. I am doing away with you once and for all!" He is looking more monstrous by the second.

The atmosphere suddenly begins to change. The colour drains from the landscape, leaving a lacklustre greyness, and only Cecil's orange eyes stand out starkly. The temperature drops dramatically as the air turns frosty, and my teeth begin to chatter. I feel a sense of impending doom. I am wondering what is about to happen when I see a noose hurtling towards me from Cecil's direction. My first instinct is to flee, but there is nowhere to run, and I must stand my ground. I swallow hard and remain rooted in position.

The noose positions itself a distance above my head. My hands are roughly bound behind my back by an invisible force. I watch in trepidation as the noose slowly lowers itself and encircles my neck. My body freezes. Fear has wrapped itself tightly around me like a hungry python, squeezing all hope out of me. Did my ancestors bring me this far only to abandon me and allow the enemy to triumph? Confused tears begin to stream from my eyes.

"Tears of regret, I see. That is what happens when you think too highly of yourself and overestimate your abilities. You pay the price," Cecil says, his voice laced with malice.

I plead for higher powers to intervene, but I am met with deafening silence. I am abruptly and viciously hauled up into the air by the rope before it comes to a sudden stop. I powerlessly dangle above the ground, the noose now tight around my neck, strangling me. I begin to feel constricted. I am unable to access air. My chest begins to burn. I want to exhale, gasp, cough but I am blocked. This has to be the most unpleasant feeling in the world. I start to feel light-headed and nauseous and my body begins to thrash and flail helplessly. I must be a pitiful sight. The life-force is draining out of me; I am weakening by the millisecond. My physical self is beginning to shut down. So, this is how it feels to die, to come to an ignominious end on a holy hill.

Ruva's face appears in front of me. My vision is blurry, but I can see her, crystal clear. Her face is drenched in tears, and an indescribable anguish emanates from her core. My heart splinters. I have let her down. I have failed my beloved flower. I want to comfort her as I always do when something upsets her, but I cannot. A deep shame settles within my beleaguered being. I try to mouth the words "I'm sorry" but my withering body refuses to obey me, too preoccupied with its imminent demise. It feels as if I am being repeatedly stabbed by multiple knives coated with poison. It is pure searing torment. I cannot bear it any longer. I am ready to succumb.

Then I hear Muchembere's voice.

"It is not over. Your bones shall rise again."

I see Tateguru's form swimming in my dimming line of vision. I telepathically ask him to welcome me with open arms when I join him on the other side. He tells me he is not willing to welcome me just yet because I have not finished my work, I still have a duty to fulfil. He stretches out his hand and touches the rope, and the noose immediately loosens, releasing me from its stranglehold. I gently fall to the ground. I hear Cecil shout out profanities in frustration – his effort to destroy me has been thwarted yet again.

I lie on the rocky ground for what seems an interminable length of time, trying to regain my strength. I am more than ready for this whole ordeal to be over. I have twice looked death squarely in the eye in a relatively short span of time, and the novelty has worn off.

Tateguru says, "You are almost there, my daughter. Summon all the energy within your being, rise and bring this chapter of our history to its long overdue close. Nyikadzimu is banking on you. The time has come to cast out the evil trespassing spirit that has haunted our land for too long. Finish this decisively." And then he is gone.

From a source I cannot identify, I hear the sound of a *ngoma* playing. The thumping drumbeat stirs something primal inside me. It is followed by the rattling sound of *hosho* that shakes my inner world. I am revived. When the hallowed sound of the *mbira* joins in, a bonfire is promptly lit within my being. I am ignited by this indigenous orchestra. I feel electrified. My body lifts itself from the ground and begins to move of its own accord, leading me how it sees fit. It is moving in ways I did not think it capable of. It is effortlessly aligned to the rhythm of the music. This dance feels centuries old, like an inheritance that was patiently waiting for its moment of revelation. I can feel myself leaping as if to greet the sky. I am convinced I have grown wings. Or maybe it is simply my spirit soaring with jubilation. I abandon myself completely to the movements of my body. I finally know what authentic freedom feels like. It is every limb in unbridled motion at the speed of sound. It is ecstatic rhythm. It is the opposite of inertia. It is sweat mingling with ancient tears to cleanse polluted blood. It is ancestral rage embodied. It is a release and a reckoning. It is a ritual dance of reclamation on the land's most sacred site.

As my bare feet pound the ground, Malindadzimu seems to respond to me. The hill is shaking and moving in tandem with my dancing. I feel tremors rising from the ground and coursing through my body. Is it possible that I am somehow rocking the very foundations of this venerated space? The surrounding kopjes are awake and pulsating. I can swear the boulders are singing liberation songs. My heart of stone is uniting with these mystical granite hills to achieve a common aim – to vomit out the colonial poison and heal a nation in crisis. We are committed allies, and together we are a formidable force. This is guerrilla spiritual combat at its purest; the raw enactment of mystical warfare.

I hear a voice that I recognise as belonging to Murenga say, "*Mupambepfumi ibvu munyiku yedu. Tora zvako zvese, usadzoke zvakare.*" He is instructing the coloniser to leave our land with all his belongings and never return. Murenga's words are followed by the earth-shattering sound of his elephant trumpeting, and then Cecil's grave explodes into pieces. I am so startled that I immediately stop dancing. I reflexively check to see if I have been harmed by the explosion. As I do this, I feel aftershocks underneath my feet. Satisfied that I am alright, I turn my stunned attention to what used to be Cecil's grave. I look over at Cecil. His features are now grotesquely distorted. He lets out a mangled scream and sinks to his knees. All the prior arrogance and menace are gone; he looks like a defeated spirit.

While I am still trying to process what has just occurred, there are two other explosions in quick succession. A pair of tombs of colonial officials situated near Cecil's grave have also been destroyed. A nearby memorial housing the remains of a settler patrol killed by Ndebele warriors during the first African revolt against colonialism in Rhodesia proceeds to break apart, collapse and also explode. In that same instance, I see a vision of the statue of a Scottish missionary located at the majestic Mosi oa Tunya Falls between Zimbabwe and Zambia – which he needlessly named Victoria Falls after British Queen Victoria when he stumbled upon it – tumbling down from its pedestal and shattering on the ground. This is ancestral wrath in action, the guardians of the land are decimating the legacy of the usurpers.

The ghosts of empire gather around Cecil. Their misery is vivid. Their despondent wails of despair permeate the atmosphere. I watch them as they mourn the death of Rhodesia, keening with grief. I think of the wailing of the dispossessed skeletons Cecil and I encountered at the hotel in Nyanga, and the way Cecil addressed them with utter contempt. How the tables have turned. There is a saying I grew up hearing: "Life is a wheel, it always turns." Now Cecil is the one weeping pathetically on his knees surrounded by his powerless comrades. Rhodesia has been conquered. The once indomitable Rhodesians have been toppled from their dizzyingly high places. Rhodesia is no longer a living system; it is nothing more than a decomposing carcass. With the aid of the mighty ancestral spirits, I have killed Rhodesia as I vowed I would. Now our land can author its own story instead of mechanically following an imposed and toxic script.

The metal door from earlier appears behind Cecil and his band of colonial phantoms, and they begin to be violently pulled one by one into it. They make desperate attempts to resist, but these are ultimately in vain. A cool refreshing breeze wafts through my being as I watch them being dragged through the open door. The last one to go is Cecil.

"Please," he begs, his hand stretched towards me in a last-ditch appeal.

He is now unrecognisable, his degeneration so severe. He no longer resembles his former imperial self, he is nothing more than a wretched goblin now. I shake my head, and he lets out one final cry of anguish before the door swallows him hungrily. It then slams shut and disappears. It is done.

The taste of emancipation floods my mouth, and I savour it with satisfaction. The rightful has at last triumphed over the invasive. The heavy padlock on the minds and souls of the land's inhabitants has been unlocked. The sorcery has been reversed and the mass hypnosis undone. Murenga's elephant trumpets again, but this time the sound is celebratory. As I am basking in victory, the sky begins to pour down buckets of rain. One moment I am dry, the next I am soaked. The floodgates have been unleashed, the heavens approve.

I hear Muchembere's voice in my ear. "This is cleansing rain, washing away any remaining pollutants and impurities. It is raining all across the land. Go to one of the caves and shelter there until it stops. Then you are free to return home. You have diligently carried out your first assignment. More work awaits you in the future, but for now, you can exhale and congratulate yourself for a job well done. You have lived up to our belief in you."

I thank her and my other ancestors and spirit guardians then scamper to find the nearest cave. The thought of reuniting with my mother and daughter fills me with indescribable joy. The experience has been taxing and arduous but completely worth it. I look forward to what the future brings. I know I am fully equipped to handle anything that may come my way because I walk with a sacred multitude. My destiny has been activated, and I am ready to shoulder all its power and pain until its fulfilment and conclusion.

As soon as the rain ceases, I emerge from the cave and take one last delighted look around my surroundings before stamping my sceptre on the ground. I am teleported to our yard at home. It is dusk, my favourite time of day. I take a deep breath before opening the front door.

Mother and Ruva are sitting side by side on a sofa in the living room. Anxiety permeates the space. At the sight of me, Ruva leaps up and rushes into my open arms. Mother stands up and starts thanking the Lord at the top of her voice.

"Mhamha I was so worried about you!" Ruva says. "You didn't come back from work, and we couldn't reach you on your phone. We thought something bad had happened to you, that maybe the white man at the gate had done something awful to you. There was a time I saw you in front of me, you were in so much pain and struggling to breathe. I thought I had lost you forever!" She is feverish with emotion.

I hold her close as tears begin to cascade down my cheeks.

"I'm sorry you had to see something so terrible, Ruva. I'm alright; you haven't lost me. There's no need to worry anymore, okay?"

I look over at Mother.

"We thank God you are back safe and sound. We were fearing the worst. I almost went to report you missing at the police station, but my intuition kept telling me to wait, that you would return intact. And now here you are. I am so relieved. But what happened to you, where were you? And what are you wearing?" Mother eyes me curiously.

I sigh. "It's a long and complicated story. I'll explain everything once I've rested and gathered myself."

"Okay. The important thing is you are back home with us. Ruva was a wreck without you. We both were. It's been an odd couple of days. On the news they are reporting that the missing Zimbabwe Bird has mysteriously returned, and the grave of Cecil John Rhodes has exploded. The authorities are investigating how this all happened. Strange things are taking place," Mother says.

I shift uncomfortably. She has no idea just how strange, but she will know soon enough. I tighten my grip on my sceptre and on my embrace of Ruva.

Acknowledgements

My heartfelt thanks go to my family for their support, patience and presence during the period I wrote this book. Even though times were heavy, they held me up and kept me going. Without my family to count on, this book would not exist. I owe them every single sentence.

I am infinitely grateful to Samantha Rumbidzai Vazhure for believing in my story and affording it the honour of publication. It is because of her that the words and message in this book will be read and absorbed by others. For a writer, there is no greater gift than this. My gratitude is immeasurable.

I am deeply thankful to Lazarus Panashe Nyagwambo for the incisive, pertinent and keen-eyed editing that elevated my rough story into an actual book worthy of being read. Your input is greatly appreciated.

Profound thanks also go to Memory Chirere for encouraging me to pursue this story when doubt kicked in. Your encouragement was the lifeline I needed to carry on until completion.

About the author

Cynthia is a Zimbabwean author and poet. She is the granddaughter of Shona novelist J.W. Marangwanda, one of the earliest published African writers during Zimbabwe's colonial period. Cynthia is a well-known spoken word poet and slam poet, performing since 2008. She has performed in Zimbabwe, Namibia, The Netherlands, Lesotho, Germany and South Africa. Her poems have been published in several anthologies and literary magazines. She is the recipient of a Zimbabwe National Arts Merit award for Outstanding First Creative Published Work for her debut novella *Shards* in 2015. Her work is concerned with the intersections and conflicts between the traditional and the modern, the local and the global, the spiritual and the material.